[美] 玛丽...

05

NIGHT OF THE NINJAS

忍者的秘密

主译:蓝葆春　蓝纯

湖北长江出版集团
湖北少年儿童出版社

★ 名人推荐 ★

陈乃芳：美国麻省大学高级访问学者，曾任驻比利时使馆兼驻欧盟使团教育处参赞，北京外国语大学校长；第九、十届全国政协委员，政协外事委员会委员，中国高等教育学会高教管理研究会副理事长，中国教育国际交流协会常务理事，《国际论坛》杂志主编；由泰国王储授予名誉教育学博士、由英国兰卡斯特大学校长亚历山大公主授予名誉法学博士，并有多部论著。

亲爱的少年读者们：

你们好！最近我有机会阅读了一套英汉双语版的系列丛书，名字叫做《神奇树屋》(Magic Tree House)，作者是当今美国最著名的少儿读物作家之一——玛丽·波·奥斯本。几乎全美国的少年儿童都喜欢读她写的《神奇树屋》，把她当作自己的好朋友。我虽早已年过六旬，但是我和美国的小朋友们一样，一拿到这套书就爱不释手，不到两天就全部读完了。

你们也许要问：您为什么这么喜欢这套书呢？

我的回答是：首先，作者的创作思路紧紧扣住了小读者渴求知识、喜欢冒险、充满好奇和富于幻想的心理特点，成功地打造了神奇树屋这个平台。神奇树屋挂在森林里最高的一棵橡树的顶上，里面堆满了图书。它的神奇之处在于小读者翻开其中的任何一本书，指着书中的一幅插图许愿说"我希望到那里去"，梦想就能即刻实现。其次，作者充分发挥"魔法"的作用，轻松自如地引领读者穿越时空，周游世界。从见识白垩纪恐龙时的翼龙和冰河时代最凶猛的野兽剑齿虎，到体察今日的澳洲袋鼠；从了解美国早期荒凉西部的牛仔生活，到欣赏古代中国牛郎织女的传奇故事；从游览古埃及的金字塔到身陷2000多年前中国的秦始皇陵；从遭遇加勒比海的海盗到拜会东方的日本忍者；从历险维苏威火山的爆发到探秘亚马孙河的热带雨林……真是随心所欲，神游八方。再者，作者成功地塑造了杰克和安妮这一对小兄妹，通过他俩的所见、所闻、所思、所想和亲身历险，把历史故事、神话传说、科普知识、人文传统等栩栩如生地展现在读者面前，让你如同身临其境。最后，这套书不仅内容丰富有趣，而且文字浅显易懂，让人捧读之下，不忍释手。

为了把这套优秀的少儿读物介绍给全中国的中小学生，湖北少儿出版社特别邀请了我的老同学、老同事、老朋友蓝葆春爷爷和他的女儿——北京外国语大学的蓝纯教授负责全套丛书的汉语翻译。他们的译文既忠实于原文，又琅琅上口。所以我建议小读者们在阅读过程中先读译文，再读原文，这样一书两用，既增长了知识，又提高了英语，算是一举两得吧。

最后我想感谢两位译者请我作序，让我有了先睹为快的机会。也感谢湖北少儿出版社为全中国的中小学生们献上的这份大礼。

祝你们阅读愉快！

陈乃芳

目录

1

回到树林 *1*

2

打开的书 *9*

3

咦——嗨！ *15*

4

被俘 *23*

5

雾中的火光 *33*

6

影子武士 *41*

7

走向东方 *49*

8

险滩 *59*

9

鼠道 *67*

10

晚安，小豆子 *75*

回到树林

Back into the Woods

可是安妮已经消失在树林里了。

杰克望着树林。他觉得没什么希望，也许他再也见不到莫根了。

　　"咱们再去看看吧，杰克！"安妮说。

　　杰克和安妮正从图书馆回家，那条路恰好经过蛙溪湾树林。

　　杰克叹了口气。"我们今天早晨刚刚去看过了，"他说，"前天我们也去了，大前天也去了。"

　　"那你就别去，"安妮说，"我自己去。"

　　她一下子钻进了树林。

　　"安妮，等等！"杰克喊着，"天快黑了！我们得回家！"

　　可是安妮已经消失在树林里了。

　　杰克望着树林。他觉得没什么希望，也许他再也见不到莫根了。

　　都过去几个星期了，树林里没有一点莫根·拉菲的踪迹，也不见树屋的影子。

　　"杰克！"安妮在树林里喊，"它回来了！"

　　啊，肯定又像往常一样，安妮在假装，杰克心想。可是他的心跳还是开始加速。

　　"快过来！"安妮喊道。

"她最好别跟我开玩笑。"杰克嘟哝了一句。

他钻进树林去找安妮。

夜幕已经降临,蟋蟀在唧唧地叫着,树林里什么也看不清。

"安妮!"杰克喊道。

"这儿呢!"安妮回答。

杰克继续往前走。"这儿是哪儿?"他反问。

"这儿就是这儿!"

安妮的声音从上方传来。

杰克抬头一看。

"啊,嗬!"他深吸了一口气。

安妮正从树屋的窗口向外招手。那树屋搭在树林里最高的一棵橡树上,一架长长的绳梯从上面垂下来。

神奇树屋又回来了。

"快上来吧!"安妮喊道。

杰克向绳梯跑去,迫不及待地往上爬。

他爬呀,爬呀,爬呀!

杰克向上爬的时候,仰头向树林上方看了一眼,发现树顶上方的天空还是亮的。

他终于爬进了树屋。

安妮正坐在阴影里，书撒了一地。

地板上的字母"M"在黑暗中发着微光。M 代表莫根·拉菲。

但还是没有莫根的踪影。

"我想知道莫根到底在哪儿！"杰克说。

"也许她去图书馆拿其他的书了。"安妮说。

"我们刚才就在图书馆，应该能碰到她的呀，"杰克回答，"再说图书馆现在也关门了。"

吱吱！

有只小老鼠从书堆后面跑了出来，跑到地板上闪闪发光的字母 M 那儿。

"呀！"安妮惊讶地叫出了声。

那只小老鼠坐在 M 的正中间，抬头注视着杰克和安妮。

"啊，真可爱！"安妮说。

杰克也不得不承认那只老鼠的确很可爱。它毛色灰白，一双大眼睛又黑又亮。

安妮慢慢地伸出手，小老鼠并不跑开。安妮轻轻地拍了拍它的小脑袋。

"你好，小豆子，"她说，"我可以叫你小豆子吗？"

"哦，又来这一套！"杰克咕哝着。

"你知道莫根在哪儿吗？"安妮问老鼠。

吱吱。

"你疯了，安妮，"杰克说，"虽然它是树屋里的老鼠，但这并不能证明它也有魔法。它不过是一只从外面爬进来的普通老鼠而已。"

杰克又向四周看了看，发现地上有一张纸。

"那是什么？"他问。

"什么什么？"安妮反问。

杰克走过去捡起那张纸，纸上面写着字。

"噢，天呐！"杰克念完那些字，轻声叫了出来。

"是什么？"安妮问。

"一张便条，"杰克说，"肯定是莫根留下的。我想她遇到大麻烦了！"

打开的书

The Open Book

"对，"杰克说，"我想知道她是不是还留下了其他的线索。"他把树屋扫视了一遍。

"你看那儿！"安妮指着角落里的一本书说，"那是唯一一本打开的书。"

杰克把那张纸条给安妮看。上面写着：

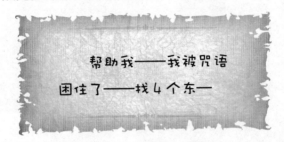

帮助我——我被咒语
困住了——找4个东一

"啊，不好!"安妮说，"我们得去救她。可是'东'是什么呢？"

"也许莫根是想写'东西'这个词，"杰克说，"你看'东'字后还有一道横线，像是'西'字的第一笔。"

"也许那咒语正使她消失，或者别的什么。"安妮说。

"对，"杰克说，"我想知道她是不是还留下了其他的线索。"他把树屋扫视了一遍。

"你看那儿！"安妮指着角落里的一本书说，"那是唯一一本打开的书。"

杰克又四处看了一遍。安妮说得对，他禁不住打了个寒战。

杰克走过去把书拾了起来，拿到窗前。西下的夕阳把书照得金黄金黄的。

　　杰克注视着书页上的那幅画，画里有许多开着白花的树。那些树长在一座山的侧面，旁边是一条又宽又急的河流。

　　画里还有两个人，穿着黑衣服，戴着黑面罩，背上插着两把长剑。

　　"天呐！"杰克嘀咕着。

　　"他们是什么人？"安妮问。

　　"我想是日本忍者！"杰克回答。

　　"日本忍者？真的吗？"安妮问。

　　"莫根把书翻到这一页留在树屋里，肯定有原因。"杰克说。

　　"也许那就是咒语起作用时她所在的地方。"安妮应道。

　　"或者是那四件东西所在的地方！"杰克说。

　　"咱们走！"安妮喊道。

　　"现在？"杰克问。

　　"是呀，莫根遇到麻烦了！她现在需要我们！"安妮说。

　　"可是我们要先看看这本书呀，"杰克说，"这样才能做好准备。"

　　"不行！"安妮说，"时间最要紧！"她从杰克手上一把抢走了书。

"把书还给我，"杰克喊道，"我们得先了解一下那地方的情况。"

安妮把书举起，不让杰克抓到，"我们到了那儿再了解也不晚。"

"我们连那个地方在哪儿都还不知道呢！"杰克说。

可是安妮立刻就指着那幅画说："我希望我们能去这儿。"

橡树的叶子开始抖动。

吱吱！

"别害怕，小豆子。"安妮说着把老鼠抱起来，放进运动衫的口袋里。

风开始刮了。

风刮得越来越厉害。

树屋开始旋转。

越转越快！

杰克紧闭着眼睛。

然后一切都静止了。

完全的静止。

只剩下流水的声音。

咦——嗨！

E—hy!

"咦——嗨！"那个忍者吆喝了一声，向这棵树猛冲过来。另一个忍者在后面紧跟着。

"噢，天呐！"安妮惊叫。

杰克睁开眼睛。

安妮已经在向窗外张望。那只小老鼠也从她的口袋里往外偷看。

杰克向窗外望去，空气清新而凉爽。

树屋落在一棵开满白花的树上。这棵树在山侧的树林里，旁边有一条向山下奔流的小河。

两个日本忍者正站在水边的岩石上，注视着下面的山谷。

这两个忍者一高一矮，穿着黑色的上衣和裤子，头上缠着黑头巾，背上插着剑。

这场景和书上那幅画一模一样。

杰克蹲在窗户下面。

"小心，"他低声地说，"别让他们瞧见你。"

"为什么不能让他们瞧见？"安妮低声问。

"他们可能会把我们当成敌人。"杰克小声说。

安妮在杰克身边蹲下来。

杰克扶了扶眼镜，他要看看那本关于日本忍者的书。

他捡起书，翻到开头，读道：

那些被称为日本忍者的人都很神秘。

历史学家认为这些忍者生活在 14 至 17 世纪的日本。

男人和女人都能当忍者。

他们有时为保卫家族而战,有时被军阀雇用做间谍。

"哇,"杰克轻声说,"我们来到几百年前的日本了。"

他打开背包,掏出笔记本和铅笔——他喜欢做笔记——写道:

忍者就是古代日本的武士。

"杰克，"安妮轻声说，"他们正在往上看。我觉得他们知道我们在这儿。"

杰克趴在窗台上偷偷瞄了一眼。他的视线正好撞上那个高个儿忍者的黑眼睛。

"咦——嗨!"那个忍者吆喝了一声，向这棵树猛冲过来。另一个忍者在后面紧跟着。

"噢,天呐!"安妮惊叫。

"我们得快跑!"杰克说,"宾夕法尼亚的书在哪儿?"

他和安妮急忙四处寻找。

可是,那本画着宾夕法尼亚的书在哪儿呢? 那书上有蛙溪湾树林的画,没有它杰克和安妮就回不了家。

"哪里都没有!"安妮喊着。

"我们得想别的办法。快!"杰克说,"把绳梯扯起来!"

他和安妮抓住绳梯的顶端,把梯子拖进了树屋。

可是高个儿忍者往树干上一跃,

噌噌噌地开始往上爬！矮个儿忍者紧跟在后。他们像猫一样地往上爬着。

　　杰克和安妮躲在角落里，缩成一团。

　　两个忍者爬进了树屋。谁也没有开口说话。

被俘！ Gaptured

唔，不好，杰克心想，他们是不是成了俘虏？

"我们？要我们跟你们走？"安妮问。

　　两个忍者脱下手上的铁手套，手套上面有像爪子一样的
钉子。

　　"他们就是用这个爬树的。"安妮小声对杰克说。

　　两个忍者的黑眼睛警觉地盯着杰克和安妮。他们的脸上
蒙着头巾。

　　杰克被他们的眼神吓呆了。

　　安妮没被吓倒。她站起来，朝他们走过去。

　　"你们好！"她说。

　　忍者没有回答。他们像杰克一样，呆在那儿一动也不动。

　　"我们在想办法营救我们的朋友莫根。"安妮说。

　　她拿出了莫根的便条。

　　高个儿忍者从她手中接过便条看了一眼，递给矮个儿忍
者。

　　两人交换了一下眼神，然后回头审视着杰克和安妮。

　　矮个儿忍者点了一下头，把便条装进了上衣口袋。

　　"你们能帮助我们吗？"安妮问。

　　两个日本忍者没吭声。杰克多么希望自己能看到他们脸
上的表情。现在他根本无法知道那两个忍者在想什么。

矮个儿忍者把绳梯抛出了树屋。

高个儿忍者指指放下的绳梯,又指指杰克和安妮。

唔,不好,杰克心想,他们是不是成了俘虏?

"我们? 要我们跟你们走? "安妮问。

高个儿忍者点了点头。

"啊,朋友! "安妮说。

啊,朋友? 她疯了吧? 杰克心想。

矮个儿忍者沿着绳梯往下爬。他只是用双手抓住梯子,双脚根本就不碰绳梯的横档。

高个子也是这样下。

杰克惊讶得长大了嘴巴。两个忍者下得非常快,就像蜘

蛛从网上往下掉似的。

"哇!"安妮感叹道。

"现在我们有机会离开这儿了,"杰克说,"快!"他又在树屋四处找了一遍。那本宾夕法尼亚的书在哪儿呢?

"咱们跟他们走吧,杰克!"安妮说。

"不行!这不是玩游戏!"杰克回答。

"可是我觉得他们知道一些莫根的事情!"安妮说。

她开始下绳梯了。

"回来!"杰克喊道。

可是已经来不及了。

杰克叹了一声。"为什么这种事总是发生?"他问自己。

"快来,杰克!"下面传来安妮的声音。

杰克把笔记本和关于忍者的书放进背包,扶了扶眼镜,也开始下绳梯。

杰克落到地面,跟安妮一起随着忍者往外走。

太阳落到小山后面了。晚霞将天空映成金红色。

小老鼠从安妮的运动衣口袋里往外偷看。

"别怕,小豆子,"安妮低声说,"我们会照顾你的。"

你真伟大,杰克心里嘀咕。可是谁来照顾我们呢?

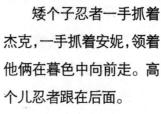

矮个子忍者一手抓着杰克,一手抓着安妮,领着他俩在暮色中向前走。高个儿忍者跟在后面。

"我们这是要去哪儿?"杰克问。

两个武士在宽阔的小河旁停了下来。河水从山

坡上奔流而下，哗哗作响。

矮个子忍者看了看杰克和安妮，放开了他俩的胳膊，把他们推到小河边。

"你要我们过河吗？"安妮大声问道。

高个子忍者点了点头。接着他和矮个儿忍者踏进奔流的小河，开始涉水过去。

"咱们跑回树屋吧！"杰克说。

"不，我们得跟着他们！"安妮说，"为了莫根！"

杰克深吸了口气。安妮说得对。

安妮抓着杰克的手，他们一起下了水。

"呀！"他俩尖叫一声，又立刻从水里跳了出来。

杰克觉得这是他接触过的最冷的水，比冰还冷，冷得刺骨。

"我不能下水！"安妮浑身发抖。

"我也不能下去，"杰克说，"我会得心脏病的。"

两个忍者回头看了看杰克和安妮，趟水而回。

高个儿忍者抓住杰克。

"救命呀！"杰克大叫。

没想到那忍者把杰克高高地举了起来，放在肩上。

矮个儿忍者则把安妮放在肩上。

然后两个忍者又踏进小河里。冰冷而湍急的河水在他们周围打着漩涡。河水淹到了矮个儿忍者的腰。

可两个忍者在小河中走起来就像两只航行的船一样平稳。

5

雾中的火光

Flames in the mist

"谁举着火把?"安妮问。

杰克上气不接下气,根本说不出话。何况他也不知道举火把的是谁。

水越来越浅。不一会儿他们就上了岸。两个忍者把杰克和安妮放到地上。

"谢谢!"安妮说。

"谢谢!"杰克说。

"吱吱!"老鼠叫道。

两个忍者没有作声,只是四下张望。

杰克也看了看周围。一轮圆月正升上天空,可以看见山侧点缀着一些黑色岩石。

两个忍者又开始行动了。他们默默地穿过那些岩石,往山坡上走去。

杰克和安妮跟在他们后面。杰克现在不害怕这两个忍者了,他甚至开始喜欢他们了,也许他们真能帮助他俩找到莫根。

两个忍者走得悄无声息,可杰克和安妮却弄出许多声响。

他们气喘吁吁地走在满是岩石的山坡上,脚上的胶底运动鞋发出吱嘎吱嘎的响声。

突然,两个忍者收住了脚步。杰克看出他们的眼睛似乎在搜寻着什么。下面的山谷里传来了说话声。杰克看见火把在薄雾中闪烁。

两个忍者加快了步伐。杰克和安妮急忙跟上。

"谁举着火把?"安妮问。

杰克上气不接下气,根本说不出话。何况他也不知道举火把的是谁。

他们来到一片松树林。树林里夜鸟在鸣叫,风把树枝吹得唰唰响。

两个忍者像鬼魂一样穿过树林,他们的身影在月色和树影中时隐时现。

杰克和安妮拼命跟上。

终于,忍者停了下来。

其中一个伸出一只手,好像是叫杰克和安妮等着。接着两个忍者一起走进树林深处,不见了踪影。

"他们去哪儿了?"安妮问。

"不知道,"杰克回答,"也许这本书能告诉我们。"

他把关于忍者的书从背包里掏了出来。

他一页一页地翻着,找到一幅画着洞穴的图画。

借助那轮满月的光芒,杰克读道:

　　　　忍者们有时在隐蔽的山洞里召开会议，谋划他们的秘密使命。

"啊哈，"杰克说，"我猜他们钻进了一个隐蔽的山洞。"

他掏出笔记本和铅笔，写道：

在隐蔽的洞穴里开会

　　杰克翻到下一页，看到一幅画，画上有个忍者坐在一块地毯上。他读道：

忍者们从头领那儿接受指令。
头领是个神秘而智慧的人。
他知道很多大自然的奥秘。

"哇!"杰克轻声说。

这时,两位忍者回来了。杰克赶快把书收好。

矮个子忍者向杰克和安妮打了个手势,示意他们跟上。

树影里露出一个黑洞的入口。

"那是什么地方?"安妮小声问。

"忍者的头领!"杰克小声回答。

影子武士

Shadow warrior

　　几十支蜡烛将洞内照得通亮。影子在墙上跳动。
　　在摇曳的烛光里，杰克看见一位穿黑衣服的人坐在一张编织的地毯上。

杰克和安妮跟着忍者,穿过树荫,走进洞穴。

几十支蜡烛将洞内照得通亮。影子在墙上跳动。

在摇曳的烛光里,杰克看见一位穿黑衣服的人坐在一张编织的地毯上。

那正是忍者的头领。

带杰克和安妮进来的那个忍者向头领鞠了一躬, 退到一边。

头领盯着杰克和安妮看了一会儿。

"坐!"他说。

杰克和安妮在冰冷坚硬的地板上坐下。

吱吱。

小老鼠从安妮的上衣口袋里探出头来。

"没事的,小豆子!"安妮说。

头领看了看小老鼠, 又看了看杰克。"你们是什么人? "他问。

"我叫杰克,这是我妹妹安妮。"杰克回答。

"你们来自何处? "头领问。

"宾夕法尼亚蛙溪湾。"安妮回答。

43

"你们为什么会在这里？"头领继续盘问。

"我们在设法营救我们的朋友莫根·拉菲，"杰克说，"她给我们留了张纸条。"

安妮指着矮个儿忍者说，"我们把纸条给他了。"

"'他'？啊，你们把条子给她了，"头领说，"她已经把纸条交给我了。"

"她？"杰克和安妮叫了起来。

那位矮个子女忍者的眼睛亮晶晶的。杰克想，她可能在笑。

头领把莫根的纸条拿了出来。

"也许我能帮助你们，"他说，"可是，首先你们得证明你们值得我帮助。"

这时，高个儿忍者出现了。他向头领打了个手势。

头领站起来，把莫根的纸条还给安妮。

"我们现在得离开，侍卫们离这儿很近了。"

"侍卫？"杰克重复了一句。他知道侍卫是很凶残的日本战士。

"是山谷里的那些人吗？"杰克问，"那些举火把的人？"

"是的。我们的家族正和他们开战，"头领说，"我们必须

在他们找到这儿之前离开。"

"可是，营救莫根的事怎么办？"安妮说。

头领背上长剑。

"现在我没有时间，"他说，"我必须走了。"

"我们能跟你们一起去吗？"安妮问。

"不行，我们去的地方不适合你们。你们必须自己在树林里找到回家的路。"

"就我们自己？"杰克问。

"对，你们必须自己走，还要提防那些侍卫。"

"为什么？"杰克又问。

"他们会认为你们是跟我们一伙的，"头领说，"他们不会听你们辩解，也绝不会可怜你们。"

"喔！"安妮轻声说。

"既然你们已经见过忍者的生存方式，那现在就自己实践一下吧。"

"怎么实践？"杰克问。

"记住三件事！"头领说。

"哪三件？"杰克问。

"利用大自然，变成大自然，顺从大自然。"

"我能做到！"安妮说。

杰克看着她，"你能吗？"

头领转向杰克。"你们的树屋在树林东面，那就是你们要去的方向。"他说。

怎么走？杰克思索着。我们怎么才能找到东方？

他们还没来得及问，头领就鞠躬告别了，很快消失在树影里。

高个儿和矮个儿忍者把杰克和安妮领出了洞穴。外面洒满月光。

高个儿忍者指了指那片松树林，然后他们也消失在黑暗里。

现在就剩下杰克和安妮两个人了。

走向东方

To the East

　　杰克和安妮在原地站了好一会儿。
　　安妮首先开口了。"我觉得高个子刚才指的就是东方，"她说，"我们就往那儿走吧。"

杰克和安妮在原地站了好一会儿。

安妮首先开口了。"我觉得高个子刚才指的就是东方,"她说,"我们就往那儿走吧。"

"等等,"杰克说,"我得记下点儿东西。"

他拿出笔记本,就着月光写道:

1. 利用大自然

2. 变成大自然

3. 顺从大自然

"你看,杰克,"安妮悄声说,"我像一个忍者吗?"

杰克看看安妮。她把运动衫的帽子戴在头上,将带子系紧。

看起来果然像一个忍者——一个迷你型忍者。

"好主意!"杰克也悄声说,然后他也把帽子戴上了。

"好,咱们走吧。"安妮说。

神奇 树 屋
MAGIC TREE HOUSE

　　杰克放下笔记本,和安妮一起朝着东方的那片树林走去。

　　他们在树林中穿梭,林木越来越茂密。

　　所有的树看起来都一样,这把杰克弄糊涂了。他们是在朝着正确的方向走吗?

　　"等等。"他说。

　　安妮站住了。他们打量着四周的树林。

　　"你觉得我们这是在往东走吗?"杰克问。

　　"我觉得是!"安妮说。

　　"我们不能瞎猜,"杰克说,"一定得弄准了。"

　　"怎么弄准呢?"安妮问,"我们又没有指南针。"

　　这时,杰克想起了忍者头领的话。

　　"那个头领说要利用大自然。"他说。

　　"怎么利用呢?"安妮问。

　　"等等,我想起来了……"杰克闭上眼睛使劲儿想。

　　他想起一本关于露营的书,似乎讲过。可到底讲了些什么呢?

　　杰克睁开眼睛,"有了! 首先,我们需要一根小树枝,"他说。

安妮捡起一根小树枝。"给你——"她说。

"好极了,现在我们需要一片有月光的地方。"杰克说。

"那儿——"安妮喊道。

他们走进树影之间被月光照亮的一块空地。

"现在把小树枝插在地上。"杰克说。

安妮把树枝插在地上。

"树枝的影子看起来超过了六英寸,"杰克说,"你觉得呢?"

"好像是。"安妮说。

"好,这就说明影子指向东方。"杰克说。

"真棒!"安妮赞道。

"所以那条路应该指向东方!"杰克指着一个新的方向,"至少我希望如此。"

"我们现在是真正的忍者了!"安妮说。

"是,"杰克说,"也许我们本来就是呢,走!"

他们出发了,朝着东方。他们希望那的确是东方。

不一会儿,他们就出了那片松树林,走下布满岩石的山坡。他们慢慢地从一块岩石向另一块挪动,后来他们靠着一块巨

石休息。

　　"咱们再测一下方向吧。"杰克说。

　　安妮把另一根树枝插进土里。

　　"你看，"她指着地面上的影子，"那边——"

　　安妮从岩石上方偷偷地往山下看。

"呀！"她小声叫了一声。

杰克也往下看。他的心脏几乎停止了跳动。

燃烧着的火把正往山上走。是侍卫！

杰克和安妮躲到岩石后面。

吱吱,小老鼠叫着。

"安静,小豆子！"安妮说。

杰克把手伸进背包,掏出那本关于忍者的书。

"说不定书中的一些知识能帮助我们。"他说。

杰克一页页地翻着书,总算找到了他要找的东西。那是
一张穿着竹铠甲的士兵的画,那些士兵都拿着剑。他读道:

侍卫是凶残的日本
战士,他们身佩两把杀敌
的利剑。

安妮拍了一下杰克的肩膀。

杰克看看她。

安妮指指山上。

一个身影正向他们走来，离他们已经很近了。

他的竹制铠甲在月光下闪闪发光，他的两把利剑也亮得吓人。

来者是个日本封建时代的侍卫。

险滩

Dragon Water

他们朝东方走去。他们绕过岩石，来到山脚，一直走到那条宽阔而冰冷的小河旁才停下来。

河水似乎比原来更宽了。

杰克和安妮蹲在一起。侍卫们就在他们两侧。他俩被包围了！

杰克紧靠着岩石。

那个侍卫左瞧瞧，右看看，一点点地逼近他们。

杰克屏住呼吸。

"变成大自然！"安妮小声说。

"什么？"杰克小声问。

"变成大自然，变成一块岩石。"

哦，这太荒唐了，杰克心想。

可他还是紧闭双眼，尽力变成岩石的一部分。

杰克尽力让自己变得像岩石一样静止、坚固、寂静。

没过多久他就觉得自己真的像岩石一样坚强而安全了。他真想永远变成一块岩石。

吱吱。

"他走了，"安妮说，"他们都走了。"

杰克睁开眼睛。那个侍卫走了。杰克站起来，朝岩石那边看去，火把也都不见了。

"咱们走吧！"安妮说。

杰克深吸了一口气。他觉得自己很了不起——他变得越来越像一个忍者了，甚至像一个忍者头领。

"继续向东！"他说。

他们朝东方走去。他们绕过岩石，来到山脚，一直走到那条宽阔而冰冷的小河旁才停下来。

河水似乎比原来更宽了。

"我没看见树屋啊。"安妮说。

杰克望着小河那边黑色的树林。月光照着林间苍白的花朵。可是树屋在哪儿呢？

"我也没看见树屋，"杰克说。"我们得先过河，然后再设法找到树屋。"

水撞击着岩石奔流而下，发出哗哗的响声。

吱吱。小老鼠从口袋里往外偷看。

安妮轻轻拍着老鼠的小脑袋说，"别害怕，像我们一样，做个忍者。"

"咱们走吧！"杰克说。

他深吸了口气，踏进小河。冰冷的河水打着漩儿，淹没了他的膝盖。急流把他冲倒了。

杰克紧紧抓住岸边的草。河水还在他周围打着漩儿。

他冻得要死!

"杰克!"安妮抓住他的双臂,把他拉回岸上。

"好险哪!"安妮说。

杰克擦干眼镜。幸好眼镜没有掉进水里。

"你没事儿吧?"安妮问。

"不——不行了!"杰克说。他冻得牙齿咯咯直响,骨头都凉透了。

"我们过不了河,"安妮说,"再试一次我们就会被淹死的。"

"不淹死也会冻死!"杰克说。

他把运动衫的帽子扯了下来。他再也不觉得自己像个忍者了。

安妮也把自己的帽子扯了下来。她叹口气说,"我们怎么办?"

吱吱。

小豆子爬出安妮运动衫的口袋,跳到地上。

小老鼠跑开了。

"小豆子,回来!"安妮喊着。

"别喊了，"杰克说，"我们跟着小豆子走吧。"

"为什么？"安妮问。

"我们得照头领说的去做！"杰克说，"顺从大自然！"

"啊，对！"安妮说，"跟着小豆子！可是它去哪儿了？"

月光下，杰克看到了小老鼠，它正沿着河岸在草丛中奔跑呢。

"在那儿！"他叫道，"快跟上！"

安妮慌忙跟上杰克。他们紧紧跟着小豆子，在湍急的河边跑着。

在月光的照耀下，他们看到一截掉下来的树枝正好横跨在河水最窄的地方，树枝两端就架在河的两岸。

小老鼠向树枝跑去。

"小豆子正在过桥呢！"安妮说着就要跟过去。

"等等！"杰克叫道，"我们不能在那根树枝上走，树枝太细！会断的！"

鼠道

Mouse-walk

"不行,"杰克说,"树枝太细了,我们一上去它就会断的。"

"说不定我们假装自己是老鼠就能过去呢？"安妮说。

小老鼠在河对岸的高草丛中不见了。

杰克和安妮盯着树枝。

"我们得试着过去，"安妮说，"我们不是要顺从大自然吗？"

"不行，"杰克说，"树枝太细了，我们一上去它就会断的。"

"说不定我们假装自己是老鼠就能过去呢？"安妮说。

"见鬼，"杰克说，"那也不行。"

"既然你刚才能变成一块岩石，现在你就可以变成一只老鼠，"安妮说，"像老鼠一样又小又轻又快。"

杰克深吸了口气。

"我们只能这么做，"安妮说。

"好吧！"杰克回答。

"说'吱'！"安妮说。

"你真疯了！"杰克应道。

"说一声嘛，"安妮说，"这会让你觉得自己就像一只老鼠。"

杰克哼了一声，"好吧，"他说，"吱。"

"吱吱！"安妮说。

"吱，吱，吱！"他们一起说。

"咱们走，快！"安妮说。

杰克踏上了树枝。

我又小又轻又快，他这么想着，然后就踩着树枝过去了。

他走得飞快，一心想着快点到对岸，无暇他念。

他忘了又急又冷的河水，也忘了树枝其实很细。

一转眼，杰克就到了河对面。又一转眼，安妮就在他身旁了。

他们一起大笑，倒在草丛里。

"你看，你看！树枝没被压断！"安妮说。

"我觉得树枝还是够粗的，"杰克说，"我们得用科学的方法思考问题。"

"小豆子的方法！"安妮说。

"是！"杰克笑了。他感觉棒极了。

虽然刚才在对岸掉进了河里，他身上还是湿漉漉的，可他一点儿也不在意。

杰克扶了扶眼镜，站起身，"好吧，我们现在只需要找到树屋就行了。"

"不，我们不用找了。"安妮说着指向空中。

树屋的轮廓在被圆月照亮的夜空中清晰可见。它挂在高

高的树顶上，被白色的花朵环绕。

远处传来了说话声，接着杰克看到了火苗。

"侍卫们又回来了，"杰克说，"我们得马上离开。"

"小豆子在哪儿？"安妮说，"我们不能丢下它。"

"我们必须走了！"杰克说。

侍卫们的声音越来越近，火把也越来越近了。

"快走！"杰克说着抓起安妮的手，把她拉向绳梯。

"噢，杰克——"安妮伤心地说。

"走吧！走吧！"

安妮开始上绳梯了。

杰克跟在后面。他也觉得很伤心。现在他已经喜欢上那只小老鼠了，非常喜欢。

他们向上爬呀，爬呀。

就在他们快到树顶时，杰克听到了老鼠的叫声。

吱。

"哇！"安妮嚷道，"小豆子已经在里面了！"

安妮爬进了树屋，杰克也跟着进了树屋。

他喘着气。

还有别的什么人也在树屋里。

一个黑色的身影正坐在角落里。

"你们干得不错。"那个身影说。

是那位忍者头领。

"你们照忍者的样子做了。"他说。

"我的天!"杰克嘘了一口气。

吱。

头领的手掌上托着小豆子。

"照顾好你们的小帮手!"他说着就把老鼠交给了安妮。

安妮亲了亲老鼠的小脑袋。

"把这个也拿着——"头领把手伸向杰克。

他递给杰克一块小圆石头。

"这颗月亮石会帮助你们找到失踪的朋友。"头领说。

杰克看了看石头。这就是四样东西之一吗?

"你们现在得回家了。"头领说。他捡起那本宾夕法尼亚的书交给安妮。

"您在什么地方找到的?"杰克问。

"就在这儿,"头领说,"你们之前没看见,是因为你们心里

知道必须先完成任务。"

　　"那您呢？"安妮说，"您能跟我们一起回去吗？"

　　"对，"杰克说，"我们需要您帮我们找到莫根。"

　　头领笑了，"不行，我的朋友。我必须留在这里。你们沿途还会得到帮助的，但你们必须靠自己想办法。"

　　安妮打开书，找到那幅蛙溪湾的图画。

　　她指着那幅画说："我希望我们能到那儿去。"

　　风开始吹起来了。

　　白色的花朵开始摆动。云层遮住了月亮。

　　"记住，"头领说，"保持一颗善良的心。"

　　接着他轻快地下了绳梯，消失在黑夜里。

　　"等等！"杰克喊着。他还有很多事情要问头领，关于大自然，关于忍者，关于他们的使命。

　　可是树屋开始旋转了。

　　它转得越来越快！

　　杰克把石头紧紧握在手中，紧闭双眼。

　　然后，一切都静止了。

　　完全静止。

晚安，小豆子

Night, Peanut

　　"床！给小豆子睡觉，你知道的。"安妮托起小老鼠，把它放进袜子里。

　　"晚安，小豆子！"她温柔地说。

杰克睁开眼睛。

他松开拳头,注视着手中的月亮石。小石子清澈而光滑,似乎在闪闪发光。

"我们到家了!"安妮说。

吱。

安妮和老鼠朝窗外望去。

杰克和他们一起朝窗外望去。

太阳正在远方落下。

在蛙溪湾,时间一点儿也没流逝。

他们听到邻居家的狗亨利在叫。他们听到蟋蟀在歌唱。

远处,他们看见爸爸正走出屋子,站在门廊上。

"杰克——安妮——"他喊着。

该吃晚饭了。

"来了——"安妮大声回答。

杰克转身,再次端详那块月亮石。

"我想我们已经找到四样东西中的一样了!"他说。

"明天我们再找其他三样!"安妮说。

杰克点点头。他们还有很多事情要做。

　　他把月亮石放进口袋,背上背包。

　　"准备好了吗?"他问。

　　"等一等!"安妮说着脱下一只运动鞋。她把袜子脱了下来,然后又把运动鞋穿上。

　　"你要干嘛?"杰克问。

　　"我要做一张床。"安妮说。

　　"一张什么?"

　　"床!给小豆子睡觉,你知道的。"安妮托起小老鼠,把它放进袜子里。

　　"晚安,小豆子!"她温柔地说。

　　吱。

　　"噢,真要命!"杰克咕哝了一声。

　　安妮把老鼠举到杰克跟前。

　　"亲小豆子一下吧,杰克。"她说。

　　"别傻了,"杰克喊道,"咱们该走了。"

　　"谢谢你帮助我们!"安妮对老鼠说。

　　她把小豆子轻轻放在发光的字母 M 上面,又从口袋里掏出莫根的纸条,放在老鼠的身边。

"明天见！"安妮说。她开始下绳梯。

杰克看了看老鼠，老鼠也看着他。

一时间，老鼠的双眼看起来苍老而智慧。

"下来吧，杰克！"安妮喊着。

杰克吻了一下老鼠的小脑袋。

"晚安，小豆子。"他轻声说。

然后，他也开始下绳梯。

杰克往下爬的时候，天色越来越暗了。

等他到达地面，天几乎完全黑了。

"你在哪儿？"杰克问。

"这儿。"安妮说着碰了一下杰克的手。杰克握住她的手。

"当心！"杰克说。

"你自己也当心！"安妮回答。

他们一起穿过那片凉爽、黑暗的树林。

他们走得又轻又快——像两个忍者凯旋归来。

忍者的秘密

●忍者的头领从不公开露面,他们以平常的忍者身份在组织中活动。注意哦,你碰到的任何一个忍者,都可能是个首领!

●忍者常常跟随某个君主,为君主的利益去打打杀杀。其实,真正的忍者内心是平静的,据说忍者的精神最初是来自古代的中国,他们崇尚自然,讲究身心都要与自然合一。

●忍者组织是以家族组成的,也就是说,一队忍者可能是爸爸和儿子,叔叔和侄子,或者亲兄弟姐妹!

忍者的秘密

NIGHT OF THE NINJAS

忍者的秘密

NIGHT OF THE NINJAS

CONTENTS

1 Back into the Woods 86

2 The Open Book 93

3 E—hy! 99

4 Gaptured 105

5 Flames in the mist 113

6 Shadow warrior 119

7 To the East 125

8 Dragon Water 133

9 Mouse-walk 140

10 Night, Peanut 149

Back into the Woods

"Let's look again, Jack," said Annie.

Jack and Annie were walking home from the library. The path went right by the Frog Creek woods.

Jack sighed. "We looked this morning," he said. "We looked the day before. And the day before that."

"Then you don't have to come," said Annie. "I'll go look by myself."

She took off into the woods.

"Annie, wait!" Jack called. "It's almost dark! We have to get home!"

But Annie had disappeared among the trees.

Jack stared at the woods. He was starting to lose hope. Maybe he would never see Morgan again.

Weeks had passed. And there had not been one sign of Morgan le Fay. Nor had there been one sign of her magic tree house.

"*Jack*!" Annie called from the woods. "*It's back!*"

Oh, she's just pretending as usual, Jack thought. But his heart started to race.

"Hurry!" called Annie.

"She better not be kidding," said Jack.

He took off into the woods to find Annie.

Night was falling fast. Crickets chirped loudly. It was hard to see through the shadows.

"Annie!" Jack shouted.

"Here!" she called.

Jack kept walking. "Here

where?" he called back.

"Here *here*!"

Annie's voice came from above.

Jack looked up.

"Oh man," he breathed.

Annie waved from the window of a tree house. It was in the tallest oak in the woods. A long rope ladder hung down from it.

The magic tree house was back.

"Come on up!" Annie shouted.

Jack ran to the rope ladder. He started climbing.

He climbed and climbed and climbed.

As he climbed, he looked out over the woods. High above the treetops it was still light.

At last, Jack pulled himself into the tree house.

Annie sat in the shadows. Books were scattered

everywhere.

On the floor the letter M glowed in the dim light. The M stood for Morgan le Fay.

But there was no sign of Morgan herself.

"I wonder where Morgan is," said Jack.

"Maybe she went to the library to get some more books," said Annie.

"We were just at the library. We would have seen her," said Jack. "Besides, the library's closed now."

Squeak!

A little mouse ran out from behind a stack of books. It ran to the M shining in the floor.

"Yikes," said Annie.

The mouse sat on the middle of the M. It looked up at Jack and Annie.

"Oh, it's so cute," Annie said.

Jack had to admit the mouse was cute. It had brown-and-white fur and big dark eyes.

Annie slowly reached out her hand. The mouse didn't move. Annie patted its tiny head.

"Hi, Peanut," she said. "Can I call you Peanut?"

"Oh brother," said Jack.

"Do you know where Morgan is?" Annie asked the mouse.

Squeak.

"You're nuts, Annie," said Jack. "Just because the mouse is in the tree house doesn't mean it's magic. It's a plain old mouse that crawled in, that's all."

Jack looked around again. He saw a piece of paper on the floor.

"What's that?" he said.

"What's what?" asked Annie.

Jack went over and picked up the paper. There was writing on it.

"Oh man," whispered Jack, after he read the words.

"What is it?" said Annie.

"A note," said Jack. "It must be from Morgan. I think she's in big trouble!"

The Open Book

Jack showed Annie the piece of paper. It said:

help me — Under
a tree Find 4 thin

"Oh no," said Annie. "We have to help her. But what's a *thin?*"

"Maybe she was trying to write *things*," said Jack. "See how the *n* sort of runs off the page?"

"Maybe the spell was starting to make her disappear or something," said Annie.

"Right," said Jack. "I wonder if she left any other clues." He glanced around the tree house.

"Look!" Annie pointed at a book in the corner. "That's the only open book," she said.

Jack looked around again. Annie was right. He felt a shiver go down his spine.

Jack went over to the book and picked it up. He held it near the window. Light from the setting sun was golden on the page.

Jack stared at the picture on it. In the picture were trees with white flowers. The trees were on the side of a mountain. Near a wide, rushing stream.

Two people were also in the picture. They wore dark clothes. They had black scarves over their faces. And long swords strapped to their backs.

"Oh man," whispered Jack.

"Who are they?" Annie asked.

"Ninjas, I think," said Jack.

"Ninjas? Really?" said Annie.

"Morgan must have left the book open to this page for

a reason," said Jack.

"Maybe that's where she was when the spell got her," Annie said.

"Or maybe that's where the four things are," said Jack.

"Let's go!" said Annie.

"Now?" said Jack.

"Yes, Morgan's in trouble! She needs us *now!*" said Annie.

"But we should read this book

first," said Jack. "So we'll be prepared."

"Forget it!" said Annie. "Every minute counts!" She grabbed the book from Jack.

"Give it back," he said. "We have to find out about this place."

Annie held the book out of reach. "We'll find out when we get there," she said.

"We don't even know where *there* is!" Jack said.

But Annie pointed at the picture. "I wish we could go here," she said.

The leaves of the oak tree began to shake.

Squeak!

"Don't be scared, Peanut," said Annie. She scooped up the mouse. Then she put it in the pouch of her sweatshirt.

The wind began to blow.

It blew harder and harder.

The tree bouse started to spin.

Faster and faster!

Jack squeezed his eyes shut.

Then everything was still. Absolutely still.

Except for the sound of rushing water.

E—hy!

Jack opened his eyes.

Annie was already looking out the window. The mouse peeked out of her pouch.

Jack looked out the window, too. The air was fresh and cool.

The tree house was in a tree with white flowers. The tree was in a grove of trees on the side of a mountain. Nearby a wild stream rushed downhill.

Two ninjas were standing on rocks near the water. They were staring at the valley below.

One ninja was tall. The other was short. They wore black pants and shirts. They had black scarves around their heads. And swords strapped to their backs.

It was exactly like the picture in the book.

Jack crouched below the window.

"Be careful," he whispered. "Don't let them see you."

"Why not?" Annie whispered back.

"They might think we're some kind of enemy," said Jack quietly.

Annie crouched beside him.

Jack pushed his glasses into place. *Now* he was going to look at the ninja book.

He picked up the book. He turned to the beginning. He read:

Very little is known about the shadowy warriors called ninjas.Historians believe that ninjas lived in Japan between the 14th and 17th centuries. Both men and women were ninjas. Sometimes they fought to protect their families. Sometimes warlords hired them to be spies.

"Wow," whispered Jack. "We're in Japan, hundreds of years ago."

Jack opened his backpack. He pulled out his notebook and pencil. He liked to take notes. He wrote:

ninjas were war—
riors in old Japan

"Jack," whispered Annie. "They're looking up. I think they know we're here."

Jack peeked over the windowsill. His eyes met the dark eyes of the tall ninja.

"*E-hy*" the ninja cried. He dashed toward the tree. The other ninja followed.

"Oh no!" said Annie.

"We've got to go!" Jack said. "Where's the Pennsylvania book?"

He and Annie looked around wildly.

But where was the book about Pennsylvania? It had

the picture of the Frog Creek woods in it. Jack and Annie couldn't get home without it.

"It's not anywhere!" cried Annie.

"We've got to do something. Fast!" said Jack. "Pull up the ladder!"

He and Annie grabbed the top of the rope ladder. They pulled the ladder into the tree house.

But the tall ninja leaped at the tree trunk. Then he started climbing up the tree! The short ninja followed. They climbed just like cats!

Jack and Annie huddled in a corner.

The ninjas climbed into the tree house. Neither one made a sound.

Gaptured

The ninjas pulled iron bands off their hands.

The bands had spikes like claws on them.

"That's how they climbed the tree," Annie whispered to Jack.

The ninjas stared at Jack and Annie with dark, piercing eyes. The rest of their faces were covered by their scarves.

Jack felt frozen under their stares.

Annie wasn't frozen, though. She stepped right up to them.

"Hi," she said.

The ninjas didn't say "hi" back. They didn't move at all. They were as still as Jack.

"We're trying to help our friend, Morgan," said Annie.

She held up Morgan's note.

The tall ninja took the note from her. He looked at it.

Then he gave it to the short ninja.

The two ninjas stared at each other. Then they looked back at Jack and Annie.

Finally the short ninja nodded once. He put the note into the pocket of his shirt.

"You can help us?" Annie asked.

Neither ninja spoke. Jack wished he could see their faces. He couldn't tell what they were thinking.

The short ninja tossed the rope ladder back out of the tree house. The tall one pointed down the ladder. Then he pointed at Jack and Annie.

Uh-oh, thought Jack. Were they being captured?

"Us? Go with you?" said Annie.

The ninja nodded.

"Oh boy!" said Annie.

Oh boy? Is she nuts? wondered Jack.

The short ninja darted down the ladder. He went hand over hand. His feet didn't touch the rungs of the ladder.

The tall one did the same.

Jack gasped. The ninjas moved very fast. They were like spiders dropping from webs.

"Wow!" said Annie.

"Now's our chance to leave," said Jack. "Quick!" He looked around the tree house again. Where *was* that Pennsylvania book?

"Let's go with them, Jack," said Annie.

"No! This isn't a game!" Jack said.

"But I think they know something about Morgan!" said Annie.

She started down the ladder.

"Come back!" said Jack.

But it was too late.

Jack sighed. "Why does this *always* happen?" he asked himself.

"Come on, Jack!" came Annie's voice from below.

Jack put his notebook and the ninja book into his pack. He pushed his glasses into place. And he started down the ladder.

Jack joined Annie and the ninjas on the ground.

The sun had fallen behind the hills. The sky was streaked with red and gold.

The mouse peeked out from Annie's sweatshirt pouch.

"Don't be scared, Peanut," Annie whispered. "We'll take care of you."

Great, thought Jack. *But who is going to take care of us?*

The short ninja held Jack's arm in one hand and Annie's arm in the other. He led them through the twilight. The tall ninja walked behind them.

"Where are we going?" Jack asked.

The ninjas stopped near the rushing water of the wide stream. The water roared as it raced downhill.

The short ninja looked at Jack and Annie. He let go of their arms. Then he pushed them toward the stream.

"You want us to cross it?" shouted Annie.

The ninja nodded. Then he and the short ninja stepped

into the wild stream. They started wading across.

"Let's run back to the tree house!" said Jack.

"No, we have to follow them!" said Annie. "For Morgan's sake!"

Jack took a deep breath. She was right.

Annie grabbed Jack's hand. Together they stepped into the water.

"YIKES!" They both screamed and jumped out.

It was the coldest water Jack had ever felt! It was colder than ice. It was so cold it felt like fire.

"I can't go back in," said Annie, shivering.

"Me neither," said Jack. "I'll have a heart attack."

The ninjas looked at Jack and Annie. Then they turned around and came back.

The tall ninja grabbed Jack.

"Help!" Jack cried.

But the ninja lifted Jack high into the air. And put him on his shoulder.

The short ninja put Annie on his shoulder.

Then the two ninjas stepped into the stream again. The icy wild waters swirled around them. It went up to the short ninja's waist.

But the ninjas moved through the stream as calmly as two sailing ships.

Flames in the mist

The water grew shallow again. Then they were on dry land. The ninjas lowered Jack and Annie to the ground.

"Thanks," said Annie.

"Thanks," said Jack.

Squeak, said the mouse.

The ninjas said nothing, but they looked around.

Jack looked around, too. A full moon was rising in the sky. Dark rocks dotted the side of the mountain.

Then the ninjas started moving. They went silently up the slope, between the rocks.

Jack and Annie followed them. Jack wasn't afraid of the ninjas now. In fact, he was starting to like them. Maybe they really could help find Morgan.

The ninjas moved silently. But Jack and Annie made plenty of noise.

They panted as they climbed the rocky hillside. Their

wet sneakers made squishy sounds.

Suddenly the ninjas froze. Jack could see their eyes darting around. Voices were coming from the valley below. Jack saw torches flaming in the mist.

The ninjas started moving faster. Jack and Annie hurried after them.

"Who's carrying the torches?" Annie asked.

Jack was too out of breath to speak. He also didn't have an answer.

They came to a pine forest. Night birds called out. Wind rattled the branches.

The ninjas moved like ghosts through the forest. They appeared and disappeared, through moonlight and shadows.

Jack and Annie struggled to keep up.

Finally the ninjas came to a stop.

One ninja held out his hand, as if to say, *wait*. Then both ninjas stepped away into the shadows of the trees. And were gone.

"Where did they go?" said Annie.

"I don't know," said Jack. "Maybe the book can tell us."

He pulled the ninja book out of his pack.

He turned the pages until he came to a picture of a cave.

By the light of the full moon, he read:

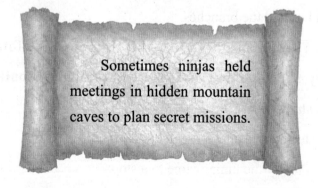

Sometimes ninjas held meetings in hidden mountain caves to plan secret missions.

"Oh man," said Jack, "I bet they went inside a hidden cave."

He pulled out his notebook and pencil. He wrote:

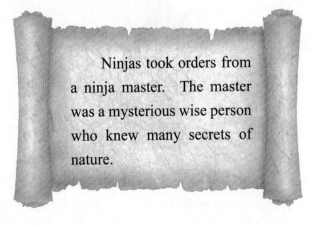

meetings in
hidden caves

Jack turned the page. He stared at a picture of a ninja sitting on a mat. He read:

Ninjas took orders from a ninja master. The master was a mysterious wise person who knew many secrets of nature.

"Wow," whispered Jack.

Just then the two ninjas returned. Jack quickly put his books away.

The short ninja motioned for Jack and Annie to follow. In the shadows was the entrance of a dark cave.

"What's in there?" Annie whispered.

"The ninja master," Jack whispered back.

6

Shadow warrior

Jack and Annie went into the cave. They followed the ninja through the darkness.

The back of the cave was lit with dozens of candles. Shadows danced on the walls.

In the flickering light, Jack saw a dark figure sitting on a woven mat.

The ninja master.

The ninja bowed to the master. Then he stepped to one side.

The master stared at Jack and Annie.

"Sit," he said.

Jack and Annie sat on the cold, hard floor.

Squeak.

The mouse poked its head out of Annie's pouch.

"It's okay, Peanut," said Annie.

The master stared at the mouse for a moment. Then he

looked at Jack. "Who are you?" he asked.

"I'm Jack and that's my sister, Annie," Jack answered.

"Where do you come from?" the master asked.

"Frog Creek, Pennsylvania," Annie answered.

"Why are you here?" he asked.

"We're trying to help our friend Morgan le Fay," said Jack. "She left us a message."

Annie pointed to the short ninja. "We gave the message to him."

"You mean, you gave the message to *her*," said the ninja master. "And *she has* given it to me."

"*She*?" said Jack and Annie together.

The woman ninja's eyes sparkled. Jack thought she might be smiling.

The master held up Morgan's note.

"Perhaps I can help you," he said. "But first you must prove yourselves worthy of my help."

Just then the tall ninja appeared. He made a sign to the master.

The master stood up. He handed Morgan's note to Annie.

"We must go now," he said. "The samurai are close."

"Samurai?" said Jack. He knew that the samurai were fierce Japanese fighters.

"Were they the ones in the valley?" Jack asked. "The ones with the torches?"

"Yes, our family is at war with them," said the master. "We must leave before they find us."

"But what about helping Morgan?" said Annie.

The master strapped on his sword.

"I have no time now," he said. "I must go."

"Can't we go with you?" said Annie.

"No, there is no place for you where we are going. You must find your way back to your house in the trees."

"Alone?" said Jack.

"Yes. You must go alone. And beware of the samurai."

"Why?" said Jack.

"They will think you are one of us," said the master. "They will ask you no questions. They will show you no mercy."

"Yikes," whispered Annie.

"But you have seen the way of the ninja. You can practice it yourselves now," said the master.

"H-how?" said Jack.

"Remember three things," said the master.

"What?" said Jack.

"Use nateure. Be nature. Follow nature."

"I can do that!" Annie said.

Jack looked at her. "You can?" he said.

The master turned to Jack. "Your tree house lies to the east. That is the way you must go," he said.

How? wondered Jack. *How do we find the east*?

Before he could ask, the master bowed. Then he disappeared into the shadows.

The two ninjas led Jack and Annie out of the cave, into the moonlight.

The tall one pointed at the pine forest. Then they too disappeared into the darkness.

Jack and Annie were all alone.

To the East

Jack and Annie stood still for a long moment.

Annie spoke first. "Well, I guess the tall ninja was pointing to the east," she said. "I guess that's the way we go."

"Wait," said Jack. "I need to write some stuff down."

He took out his notebook. In the moonlight, he wrote:

1.use nature
2.be nature
3.follow nature

"Look, Jack," whispered Annie. "Do I look like a ninja?"

He looked at her. She had pulled her sweatshirt hood over her head and tied the strings tightly.

She did look like a ninja—a very small one.

"Good idea," Jack whispered. He pulled his hood up, too.

"Okay, let's go," said Annie.

Jack put his notebook away. Then he and Annie headed east into the woods.

They slipped between trees. And more trees. And more trees.

All the trees looked the same. Jack got confused. Were they still going in the right direction?

"Wait," he said.

Annie stopped. They both stared at the woods around them.

"Do you think we're still going east?" asked Jack.

"I guess so," said Annie.

"We can't just guess," said Jack. "We have to know

for sure."

"How do we do that?" said Annie. "We don't have a compass."

Just then the master's words came back to Jack.

"The ninja master said to *use nature*," he said.

"How do we do that?" said Annie.

"Wait, I remember something——" Jack closed his eyes.

He remembered something in a camping book. *Now what was it?*

He opened his eyes. "I've got it! First we need a stick,"

he said.

Annie picked up a stick. "Here—" she said.

"Great, now we just need a space with moonlight," said Jack.

"There—" said Annie.

They moved into a moonlit space between the shadows.

"Now push the stick into the ground," Jack said.

Annie pushed the stick into the ground.

"The stick's shadow looks like it's more than six inches," said Jack. "What do you think?"

"It looks like it," said Annie.

"Okay. Then that means the shadow's pointing east," said Jack.

"Neat," said Annie.

"So *that way* is east!" Jack pointed to a new direction.

"At least I hope it is."

"We're real ninjas now!" said Annie.

"Yep," said Jack. "Maybe we are. Come on!"

They took off—heading east, they hoped.

Soon they were out of the pine woods and walking down the rocky mountainside. They moved slowly from rock to rock. Finally they rested against a giant rock.

"Let's check our direction again," said Jack.

Annie stuck another stick into the dirt.

"There," he said. He pointed to the shadow on the ground. "That way—"

Annie peeked over the rock, down the mountain.

"Yikes," she said softly.

Jack looked, too. His heart nearly stopped.

There were flames of fire coming up the mountain. The samurai!

Jack and Annie ducked behind the rock.

Squeak，said the mouse.

"Quiet，Peanut，" said Annie.

Jack reached into his pack. He pulled out the ninja
book.

"I hope something in here can help us，" he said.

Jack flipped through page after page until he found
what he was looking for. It was a picture of warriors
wearing bamboo armor. They were holding swords.
He read：

> The samurai were fierce
> Japanese fighters.
> They carried two swords
> to cut down their enemies.

Annie tapped Jack on the shoulder.

Jack looked at her.

She pointed up the mountain.

A figure was coming down toward them. He was very near.

In the moonlight, his bamboo armor was shining. His two swords were gleaming.

It was a samurai warrior!

Dragon Water

Jack and Annie crouched together. Samurai were on both sides of them now. They were trapped!

Jack pressed against the rock.

The warrior stepped closer and closer. He looked to the right. He looked to the left.

Jack held his breath.

"*Be nature,*" whispered Annie.

"What?" Jack whispered back.

"*Be nature.* Be a rock."

Oh brother, thought Jack. This was nuts. But he squeezed his eyes shut. Then he tried to be part of the rock.

Jack tried to be as still as the rock. As solid as the rock. As quiet as the rock.

Soon he started feeling as strong as the rock. As safe as the rock. He wanted to be the rock forever.

Squeak.

"He's gone," said Annie. "They're all gone."

Jack opened his eyes. The samurai warrior was gone. Jack stood up and looked over the rock. The torches were gone, too.

"Let's go," Annie said.

Jack took a deep breath. He felt great—he was getting more and more like a ninja every minute. Maybe even like a ninja master.

"East!" he said.

And they went east. Down the mountain, between the rocks. Until they came to the wide, icy stream.

The water seemed even wilder than before.

"I don't see the tree house," said Annie.

Jack looked across the stream to the dark grove of trees. Moonlight shone on their pale flowers. But where was the tree house?

"I don't see it either," said Jack. "We have to cross the water first. Then we'll try and find it."

The water was crashing and rushing over the rocks.

Squeak. The mouse peeked out from its pouch.

"Don't be afraid," said Annie. She patted the mouse's little head. "Be like us. Be like a ninja, too."

"Let's go," Jack said.

He took a deep breath and stepped into the stream. The icy water swirled up to his knees. The current knocked him over.

Jack grabbed some weeds. He held on tight as water swirled around him.

He was freezing to death!

"Jack!" Annie grabbed Jack's arms. She helped him back onto the bank.

"That was close!"said Annie.

Jack wiped his glasses. Luckily, they hadn't fallen off in the water.

"Are you okay?" said Annie.

"N-not really," said Jack, His teeth chattering. He was chilled to the bone.

"We'll never get across," said Annie. "We'll drown if we try."

"Or fr-freeze to death," said Jack.

He pulled off the hood of his sweatshirt. He didn't feel much like a ninja anymore.

Annie pulled off her hood too. She sighed. "What can we do?" she said.

Squeak.

Peanut climbed out of Annie's sweatshirt pouch and leaped onto the ground.

The mouse scampered away.

"Peanut, come back!" Annie called.

"No," said Jack. "We have to follow Peanut."

"Why?" asked Annie.

"We have to do what the master said!" said Jack. *"Follow nature!"*

"Oh. Right!" said Annie. "Follow Peanut! But where is Peanut?"

In the moonlight Jack saw the little mouse. It was running through the grass along the stream.

"There!" he cried. "Come on!"

Annie hurried after Jack. Jack hurried after Peanut. They ran beside the rushing waters.

A moonlit branch had fallen across a narrow part of the stream. It touched both shores.

The mouse was running over the branch.

"Peanut's going over a bridge!" said Annie. She star-

ted to follow.

"Wait!" cried Jack. "We can't go on that branch. It's too small! It'll break!"

Mouse-walk

The mouse vanished into the tall grass on the other side of the stream.

Jack and Annie stared at the tree branch.

"We have to *try to* cross it," said Annie. "We're supposed to follow nature."

"Forget it," said Jack. "It's too little. It'll crack in a second."

"Maybe if we pretend we're mice, we can do it," said Annie.

"Oh brother," said Jack. "Not again."

"If you could be a rock, you can be a mouse," said Annie. "Just be teeny and light and fast."

Jack took a deep breath.

"We *have to*," said Annie.

"Okay," Jack said.

"Say 'squeak,'" said Annie.

"You're nuts!" said Jack.

"Just do it," said Annie. "It'll help you feel more like a mouse."

Jack groaned. "Okay," he said. "Squeak."

"Squeak," said Annie.

"Squeak, squeak, squeak," they said together.

"Let's go! Hurry!" said Annie.

Jack stepped onto the branch.

I'm teeny. I'm light. I'm fast, he thought. Then he darted across the branch.

Jack moved so quickly, he didn't think about anything—except getting to the other side.

He forgot the wild, freezing water. He forgot the smallness of the branch.

Suddenly Jack was on the other side. Suddenly Annie was right beside him.

忍者的秘密
Night of
the
Ninjas

They laughed and fell together into the grass.

"See! See! The branch didn't break!" said Annie.

"I guess it was big enough," said Jack. "I guess we just had to think the right way."

"The Peanut way," said Annie.

"Yeah," said Jack, smiling. He felt great.

He was still wet from his fall into the stream. But he didn't mind anymore.

Jack pushed his glasses into place and stood up. "Okay, now we just have to find the tree house," he said.

"No, we don't," said Annie. She pointed up.

The tree house was outlined against the moonlit sky. High in a tree. Surrounded by white flowers.

In the distance came the sound of voices. Then Jack saw flames.

"The samurai are coming back," said Jack. "We have

神奇 树屋

MAGIC TREE HOUSE

to go."

"Where's Peanut?" said Annie. "We can't leave Peanut."

"We have to," said Jack.

The voices of the samurai were getting closer. So were their torches.

"Come on," Jack said. He grabbed Annie's hand. He pulled her toward the rope ladder.

"Oh Jack—" she said sadly.

"Go! Go!"

Annie started up the rope ladder.

Jack followed. He felt sad, too. He liked that little mouse now. He liked it a lot.

They climbed up and up.

Just before they got to the top, Jack heard it.

Squeak.

"Oh wow!" cried Annie. "Peanut's inside!"

Annie pulled herself into the tree house. Jack followed.

He gasped.

Someone else was in the tree house, too.

A dark figure was sitting in the corner.

"You have done well," the figure said.

It was the ninja master.

"You have followed the

way of the ninja," he said.

"Oh man," breathed Jack.

Squeak.

The master was holding Peanut.

"Take good care of your little helper," he said, handing the mouse to Annie.

Annie kissed the mouse's tiny head.

"And take this—" said the master. He held his hand out to Jack.

He gave Jack a small, round stone.

"This moonstone will help you find your missing friend," the master said.

Jack stared at the stone. Was this one of the four things?

"You must go home now," said the master. He picked up the Pennsylvania book and handed it to Annie.

"Where did you find it?" asked Jack.

"Here," said the master. "You did not see it before.

Because your heart knew you had a mission to complete first."

"What about you?" said Annie. "Can you come with us?"

"Yes," said Jack. "We need help finding Morgan."

The master smiled. "No, my friends. I must stay here. There will be more help along the way. But you must find the way on your own."

Annie opened the book. She found the picture of Frog Creek.

She pointed to it. "I wish we could go there," she said.

The wind started to blow.

The white flowers started to shake. Clouds covered the moon.

"Remember," the master said, "Keep a kind heart."

Then he swung silently down the rope ladder. He

disappeared into the dark night.

"Wait!" Jack called. There was so much he wanted to ask the master. About nature. About ninjas. About their mission.

But the tree house started to spin.

It spun faster and faster!

Jack gripped the stone in his hand. he squeezed his eyes shut.

Then everything was still.

Absolutely still.

Night, Peanut

Jack opened his eyes.

Then he opened his fist. He stared at the moonstone in his hand. It was clear and smooth. It almost seemed to glow.

"We're home," said Annie.

Squeak.

Annie and the mouse were looking out the window.

Jack looked with them.

The sun was setting in the distance.

No time at all had passed in Frog Creek.

They heard their neighbor's dog, Henry, bark. They heard crickets chirping.

In the distance, they could see their dad step out of their house. He stood on their porch.

"Ja-ack! An-nie!" he called.

Time for dinner.

"Com-ing!" Annie shouted.

Jack sat back on his heels. He looked at the moonstone again.

"I guess we have one of the four things," he said.

"We'll look for the other three tomorrow," Annie said.

Jack nodded. They had a lot more work to do.

He put the moonstone in his pocket.

He pulled on his pack.

"Ready?" he said.

"Wait," said Annie. She took off one of her sneakers. She pulled off her sock. Then she put her sneaker back on.

"What are you doing?" said Jack.

"I'm making a bed," she said.

"A what?"

"Bed! You know, for Peanut to sleep in." Annie picked up the mouse. She tucked it inside her sock.

"'Night, Peanut," she said softly.

Squeak.

"Oh brother," said Jack.

Annie held the mouse close to Jack.

"Kiss it goodnight, Jack," she said.

"Don't be silly," he said. "Let's go."

"Thanks for helping us," Annie said to the mouse.

She put Peanut gently down on the glowing M. She pulled Morgan's message out of her pouch. And put it next to the mouse.

"See you tomorrow," she said. Then she started down the ladder.

Jack stared at the mouse. It looked back at him.

For a moment, its dark eyes looked old and wise.

"Come on, Jack!" called Annie.

Jack kissed its tiny head.

"Night-night, Peanut," he whispered.

Then Jack headed down the rope ladder.

It got darker and darker as he went down.

By the time he stepped onto the ground, it was almost

completely black.

"Where are you?" said Jack.

"Here," said Annie. Her hand bumped his. He took it.

"Careful," he said.

"Careful yourself," she said.

Together they took off through the cool, dark woods.

They moved silently and swiftly—two shadow warriors

returning home.

图书在版编目（ＣＩＰ）数据

忍者的秘密：英、汉/（美）奥斯本著；蓝葆春，蓝纯译.—武汉：湖北
少年儿童出版社，2010.3
（神奇树屋：典藏版）
书名原文：Night of the Ninjas
ISBN 978－7－5353－4988－0

Ⅰ.忍… Ⅱ.①奥…②蓝…③蓝… Ⅲ.儿童文学—短篇小说—
美国—现代—英、汉 Ⅳ.Ｉ712.84

中国版本图书馆 CIP 数据核字（2010）第 040542 号

This translation published by arrangement with Random House Children's Books, a
division of Random House, Inc.

Book #5-**Night of the Ninjas** Text copyright ⓒ 1992 by Mary Pope Osborne

Magic Tree House™ is a trademark of Mary Pope Osborne, used under license.

著作权合同登记号：图字：17-2006-050

神奇树屋典藏版 5——忍者的秘密

原　　著：[美]玛丽·波·奥斯本
责任编辑：叶　珺
整体设计：一壹图文

出 品 人：李　兵
出版发行：湖北少年儿童出版社
经　　销：新华书店湖北发行所
印　　刷：孝感市三环印务有限责任公司

规　　格：880×1230　1/32　5 印张
印　　次：2010 年 4 月第 1 版　2016 年 7 月第 10 次印刷
书　　号：ISBN 978－7－5353－4988－0
定　　价：14.00 元

业务电话：(027)87679179　87679199
http://www.hbcp.com.cn